Lucky Wish Mouse
Starting School

Clara Vulliamy

ORCHARD BOOKS

This is Lucky Wish Mouse.

These are the ten Tinies

getting dressed.

They are very excited,

because today is a BIG ADVENTURE!

It's just too difficult to wait

for the adventure

to begin.

"Tinies! What are you doing?"

calls Lucky Wish Mouse.

"We're not ready –

come back inside!"

They finish their

breakfast . . .

. . . brush their teeth and whiskers

extra nicely,

because today . . .

. . . is their first day at school!

"Pack your things, Tinies,"

says Lucky Wish Mouse.

There are ten tiny pencil cases,

ten apples for breaktime

and ten smart new school bags.

"On with your coats,"

says Lucky Wish Mouse.

admit
one

pink
lemonade

I've lost my gloves!

I only have one shoe!

to do:
hem
trousers
make
favourite
tea

"Now, are we all ready?"

There are one, two, three,
four, five, six, seven, eight Tinies . . .

. . . BUT WHERE ARE
THE TINY TWINS?

Here they are.
They look worried.

"We don't want to go to school,"

say the Tiny Twins,

in very tiny voices.

"We want to stay at home."

"But why?"

asks Lucky Wish Mouse.

"We are too tiny!"

"We will get lost!"

"We won't know where the toilets are!"

"We won't know what to do!"

"Will anyone like us?"

"Will you find us at going-home time?"

"YES!"

says Lucky Wish Mouse.
"I shall be looking out for
my bravest Tinies!

Now quick, quick,
hurry –

let's go!"

"All aboard the school balloon!"

They arrive just in time
to join everybody else,
and meet their new teacher
at the school door.

We made these!

The Tiny Twins have SUCH a busy day.

There are so many new things to do!

They paint lots
of pictures . . .

make two fantastic hats . . .

and join in very loudly with the singing.

They almost completely learn

to do writing . . .

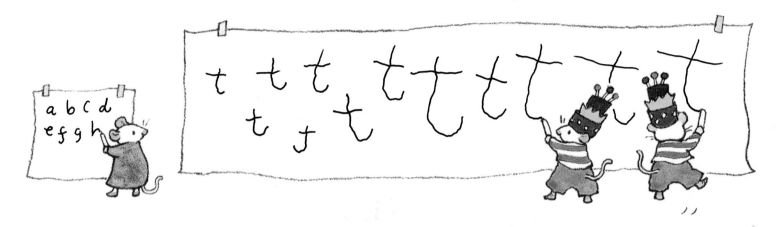

and make lots of new friends at playtime.

They even try really hard to sit still
while their teacher reads them a story.

And then it's going-home time.

There's so much to tell,

and Lucky Wish Mouse

is SO proud.

Up high, high in the school balloon,

the Tinies are making plans

for tomorrow's big adventure!

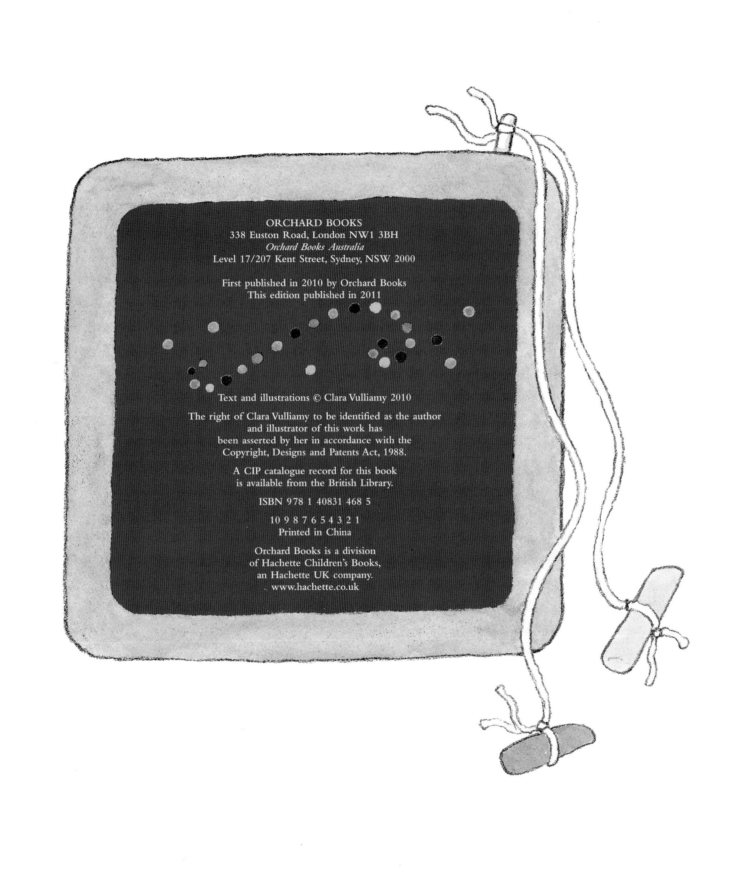

ORCHARD BOOKS
338 Euston Road, London NW1 3BH
Orchard Books Australia
Level 17/207 Kent Street, Sydney, NSW 2000

First published in 2010 by Orchard Books
This edition published in 2011

A CIP catalogue record for this book
is available from the British Library.

ISBN 978 1 40831 468 5

10 9 8 7 6 5 4 3 2 1
Printed in China

Orchard Books is a division
of Hachette Children's Books,
an Hachette UK company.
www.hachette.co.uk